Defying Gravity

Jane Anderson

A SAMUEL FRENCH ACTING EDITION

FOUNDED 1830

SAMUELFRENCH.COM
SAMUELFRENCH-LONDON.CO.UK

FOR PRODUCTION ENQUIRIES

UNITED STATES AND CANADA
Info@SamuelFrench.com
1-866-598-8449

UNITED KINGDOM AND EUROPE
Theatre@SamuelFrench-London.co.uk
020-7255-4302

Each title is subject to availability from Samuel French, depending
upon country of performance. Please be aware that *TITLE OF PLAY*
may not be licensed by Samuel French in your territory. Professional
and amateur producers should contact the nearest Samuel French
office or licensing partner to verify availability.

MUSIC USE NOTE

Licensees are solely responsible for obtaining formal written permission from copyright owners to use copyrighted music in the performance of this play and are strongly cautioned to do so. If no such permission is obtained by the licensee, then the licensee must use only original music that the licensee owns and controls. Licensees are solely responsible and liable for all music clearances and shall indemnify the copyright owners of the play(s) and their licensing agent, Samuel French, against any costs, expenses, losses and liabilities arising from the use of music by licensees. Please contact the appropriate music licensing authority in your territory for the rights to any incidental music.

IMPORTANT BILLING AND CREDIT REQUIREMENTS

If you have obtained performance rights to this title, please refer to your licensing agreement for important billing and credit requirements.

DEFYING GRAVITY was first produced by Daryl Roth at the American Place Theatre in New York City on November 2, 1997. The performance was directed by Michael Wilson, with sets by Jeff Cowie, costumes by David C. Woolard, lighting by Michael Lincoln, and orignal music and sound design by John Gromada. The Production Stage Manager was R. Wade Jackson. The cast was as follows:

TEACHER	Candy Buckley
DONNA	Sandra Daley
ELIZABETH	Alicia Goranson
MONET	Jonathan Hadary
C.B.	Philip Seymour Hoffman
ED	Frank Raiter
BETTY	Lois Smith

CHARACTERS

ELIZABETH - A five-year-old, played by an adult.
TEACHER - Her mother.
MONET - The painter.
C.B. - A mechanic on the NASA ground crew.
DONNA - A bartender in a Cocoa Beach hangout (African American)
BETTY & ED - A retired couple in their 60's.

TIME

The play takes place in 1986 and twenty years later.

AUTHOR'S NOTES

A slash (/) in the dialogue means the next speech overlaps here.

SCENE ONE

(Lights up on **MONET** *walking across the stage, carrying a portable easel, his paint box and a staff.)*

(In back of him is a projection of his painting of the Cathedral of Rouen at dusk.)

MONET. During an exhibition of my work, I watched a woman scrutinize one of my paintings. She had her face so close to the canvas, I was afraid that she would come away with a glob of paint fixed to the end of her nose. I heard her say to her companion, "I'm sorry, but there are too many colors here. I have no idea what I'm looking at." I said to her, "if you step back, Madame, perhaps you'll have a better view." She did as I suggested. "Oh, is it a building?" "Yes, It's the Cathedral of Rouen." "I live in Rouen," she said, "but this isn't what it looks like" "This is the cathedral at dawn," I said, "perhaps you were still in bed." She went to the next painting. "And what is this?" "What is the cathedral at ten in the morning." "I don't see it," she said. She went to the next. "And what about this?" "That's the cathedral at noon." "No, I still don't see it." I was about to tell the woman that she had about as much perception as a slug, when she stopped in front of a painting of the cathedral at dusk. She stared at it for a moment then said, "Yes, I recognize it now." "You must be a very late sleeper," I said. And she looked at me with a terrible sadness in her eyes, "No, Monsieur, this is the time of day when I go to light a candle for my husband."

(The projection cross-fades to an aerial view of the French countryside.)

MONET. *(cont.)* I lived long enough to see the invention of the airplane, but I never went up in one. At that time only the very brave and the very stupid were willing to fly. I once made arrangements to go up in a hot air balloon, but the fog kept us in, which was just as well because the pilot was drunk. I never saw the earth from anything higher than the bell tower of the Cathedral of Rouen. It was a wonderful view. I would have loved to have taken my paints up there, but the priest in charge was a narrow-minded wretch who believed that painters had no right to "alter the perfection of God's world." What an idiot. But I always dreamed of seeing the earth from high above. Not just a bird's eye view, but God's view. And when I died, that was the last thing I had on my mind.

SCENE TWO

(Lights up on **ELIZABETH** *as an adult.)*

ELIZABETH. The last time I saw my mother was in a visiting room next to the launch pad at Cape Canaveral. I remember we got there very early in the morning. They had donuts and hot chocolate waiting for us. Reporters kept coming in and my father bummed cigarettes from them. I asked my father if we were waiting for my mother to come back from space. He said that she hadn't even left yet. Then my grandmother gave me a coloring book and a new box of crayons to keep me busy. I broke the point on the blue crayon and I started to cry.

*(***ELIZABETH** *gets down on the floor and starts to color with crayons in front of a TV.)*

TV NEWSCASTER. *(voice over)* The space shuttle Discovery had another successful touch-down today after thirteen days in orbit. And a baby hippo was born today in the county zoo. Both mother and child are doing fine.

*(***TEACHER** *comes in and turns the TV off.)*

TEACHER. All right, Honey, time for bed.

ELIZABETH. I'm not tired.

TEACHER. Would you put your crayons away, please?

ELIZABETH. See what I did?

*(***ELIZABETH** *shows the* **TEACHER** *a piece of paper filled with crayon scribbles.)*

TEACHER. I see, that's very pretty.

ELIZABETH. You know what it is?

TEACHER. No.

ELIZABETH. It's an impressed painting.

TEACHER. A what?

ELIZABETH. You know.

TEACHER. Honey, I don't.

ELIZABETH. From the book. The painting in the book.

TEACHER. Oh, you mean Impressionist?

ELIZABETH. Yeah.

TEACHER. Honey, that's wonderful.

ELIZABETH. Guess what it is.

TEACHER. Is it a flower garden?

ELIZABETH. No.

TEACHER. Water lilies?

ELIZABETH. No.

TEACHER. Clouds?

ELIZABETH. No.

TEACHER. A sunset?

ELIZABETH. Noooo. It's spaghetti!

TEACHER. Ohhh.

ELIZABETH. *(pointing)* See?

TEACHER. I see. Come on, kiddo, it's time for bed.

ELIZABETH. I haven't touched the ceiling yet.

TEACHER. All right, are you ready?

> *(The* **TEACHER** *lifts* **ELIZABETH** *up.)*

> Did you touch anything?

ELIZABETH. No, I wasn't high enough.

> *(They do it again.)*

TEACHER. Anything this time?

ELIZABETH. Uh-uh. I have to do it again.

TEACHER. Come on, you have to reach!

> *(***ELIZABETH** *stretches her hand up and touches a planet.)*

ELIZABETH. Oh Mommy!

TEACHER. What did you touch?

ELIZABETH. The rings of Saturn.

TEACHER. What did they feel like?

ELIZABETH. Donuts!

TEACHER. You silly. C'mon, let's brush your teeth.

ELIZABETH. *(whining)* Nooo.

TEACHER. Now.

SCENE THREE

(Lights up on **BETTY** *and* **ED** *in their Winnebego. It's night and* **BETTY** *is driving.* **ED** *is holding a map and dozing.)*

(The radio is on.)

MALE RADIO ANNOUNCER. The Discovery touched down today after a successful thirteen day mission. The six crew members had a special guest on board. Ariadne the Spider, who successfully spun a web in zero-gravity. Way to go, Ariadne. In January of next year they plan to send a teacher into space. Wished they did the same with mine back in second grade. All riiight. You're listening to K-FARM 101, easy listening for the Dakotas.

BETTY. Honey, let's do that. Let's drive down to Florida and see a launch. I think we should.

ED. *(vaguely)* Florida, uh-huh.

BETTY. Are you listening?

ED. I'm listening.

BETTY. You were asleep.

ED. I'm awake.

BETTY. Are you looking for a camp ground?

ED. Yuh, uh-huh.

BETTY. You have to look for us.

ED. I am.

BETTY. I told you the other place would be full.

ED. It wouldn't of been if we had gotten there earlier.

BETTY. If we had made a reservation like I said we should.

ED. You're the one who wanted to see the Black Hills.

BETTY. What does that have to do / with anything?

ED. We don't have to go to every damn thing we see / on the map.

BETTY. We still could have called ahead. I don't know what's wrong with calling ahead.

ED. Then you should have done it.

BETTY. You wouldn't let me. Every time we passed a phone I'd want to stop and you kept saying that we didn't have to. You wouldn't listen to me and now look where we are.

ED. *(fed up)* You're right, Betty, you're absolutely right.

BETTY. You know this is also very dangerous. I could fall asleep at the wheel.

ED. You aren't going to fall asleep. You're too mad at me to fall asleep.

BETTY. I'm not mad. You're the one who's mad.

ED. I'm not mad.

BETTY. The whole point of us traveling is to see things. If you don't want to stop and look then I don't know why we're doing this, I really don't.

ED. I never said I didn't want to stop.

BETTY. You resented that we stopped for the Black Hills.

ED. Betty, the Black Hills were an extra sixty miles. I was tired of driving.

BETTY. I thought the whole point of what we're doing is to see wonderful things. If we can't stop and see wonderful things then there's no point to what we're doing.

ED. I'm tired, Betty, I'm just tired, that's all.

(a beat)

BETTY. Do you think we have a good marriage?

ED. Sure, we do.

BETTY. I'm lonely, Ed. I wish you would touch me more.

*(**ED** his arm around her **BETTY**, briefly, pats her shoulder.)*

ED. You want me to drive?

*(**BETTY** shakes her head.)*

SCENE FOUR

(The **TEACHER** *is standing in front of her class. Behind her is a projection of a cathedral.)*

TEACHER. It took an average of one hundred years to build a cathedral like this. Which means that the masons who laid the first stones could work an entire lifetime on the cathedral and never see it finished. Jason? *(a beat)* Well, actually, yes, that's true, many of the workmen were killed on the job, especially in the later years of the construction when they were working at a tremendous height. *(a beat)* Jason has brought up an interesting point, which is that some of the workmen who died were then buried in the walls of the cathedral. It was considered an honor. But no, they were not buried alive. As I was saying, it took a long time to build a cathedral and it was a very costly project. The church, which was very wealthy at the time, thought it was better to fund a cathedral than to give relief to people who were suffering from famine. Does anyone have any thoughts about that?

(No one responds.)

Well, think about it. Heather, would you change the slide?

(The projection changes to a picture of the pyramids.)

No, Honey, that's backwards.

(The projection changes a couple of times and we land on a picture of Monet's painting of the Cathedral of Rouen.)

No, you've gone too far. Back. Go back two more.

(The projection changes back to a picture of a flying buttress.)

All the towns were competing with each other to see who could build the tallest cathedral.

And for a long time you could only build to a certain height before the pull of gravity would cause the whole thing to collapse. But then in the thirteenth century they invented the flying buttress. *(a beat)* Butt, very funny. It broadened the base of the cathedral so the walls could rise hundreds of feet into the air. People always believed that if you defied gravity you were that much closer to God. Heather?

(The projection changes to the vast arched interior of a cathedral.)

Do you see? The effect it had? All the weight and stress is relieved on the outside of the building so that the inside can look like this! Do you see? Do you see how light it is? It's as if the whole interior is held up by nothing but air. And if you follow the lines of the pillars up, straight up, you are led to what many people thought was heaven. Before the airplane, this was the closest that we ever came to the experience of flight. *(a beat)* Do you think it was worth it? *(a beat)* Anyone?

SCENE FIVE

(Lights up on a bar in Florida. It's around ten at night. A lady bartender, **DONNA**, *is pouring a beer for* **C.B.**, *who's wearing a NASA cap and a two-day growth of beard.)*

*(***ED*** and ***BETTY*** are at another table near ***MONET***, who's sitting at his own table with a bottle of wine and a sketchbook.)*

C.B.. *(to* **DONNA***)* I was adjusting a bunch of nitrogen deregulators then one of the engineers shows up, tells me they changed the specifications, hands me a chart, took me an hour just to read the damn thing. Turns out they want everything back to what it was three weeks ago. These guys don't know what the fuck they're doing.

DONNA. Long day, huh?

C.B.. Oh yeah. Then I had to hassle with security so I could stay late and fix the door of my van.

DONNA. What was wrong with it?

C.B.. Hinge is broke. Every time I hit a bump the damn thing falls off. Almost wasted a jogger the other day.

DONNA. Dart board fell down again.

C.B.. Yeah, I'll take a look at it.

DONNA. What time you have to be up tomorrow?

C.B.. Three. A.M.

DONNA. What're you doin' here? You should be in bed.

C.B.. I was looking for someone to tuck me in.

DONNA. Not tonight, Sugar.

C.B.. I'm gonna work a whole lot better if I do something to clear my head.

DONNA. Try sleep.

C.B.. I'm too wound up to go to sleep.

DONNA. Uh-huh.

C.B.. Doesn't do me any good to try to sleep three hours then get up again. I might as well be doing something constructive with my time.

DONNA. Then do your laundry.

C.B.. You're breakin' my heart.

DONNA. Mine too, Baby. *(to* **ED** *and* **BETTY***)* Can I get you folks anything else?

ED. No, we're fine.

BETTY. We were wondering, are there any astronauts here tonight?

ED. Betty, I don't think so.

BETTY. *(ignoring* **ED***)* We were told that a lot of them like to come here.

DONNA. Well, most of them are in bed right now. They have kind of a big day tomorrow.

BETTY. Oh. Of course. *(to* **C.B.***)* Do you work for NASA?

C.B.. Yuh.

BETTY. *(to* **ED***)* Honey, he works for NASA.

ED. I could tell by the cap.

BETTY. *(to* **C.B.***)* We're here to see the launch.

C.B.. Uh-huh.

BETTY. It's our / first time.

ED. Are you a technician?

BETTY. *(overriding* **ED***)* We've never seen a launch before. Where do you think the best place would be to see it?

C.B.. Any where out by the highway.

ED. *(to* **BETTY***)* We have a good spot.

BETTY. Maybe he has one that's better.

ED. *(to* **C.B.***)* We're out by Cocoa Beach.

C.B.. Yeh, that's a good place.

BETTY. *(to* **DONNA***)* Are you going to see the launch?

DONNA. No Ma'am, they're too early for me. I watch the replays on TV.

ED. *(to* **C.B.***)* Think there will be a lift-off tomorrow?

C.B.. Well, it's looking pretty good. The skies are supposed to clear up.

ED. I hear you've been having / a lot of delays.

BETTY. The weather has been terrible around here hasn't it?

C.B.. Pardon me?

BETTY. The weather.

C.B.. Yeah, it's been bad.

BETTY. I hear there've been some delays.

ED. Betty, I said that already. *(to C.B.)* So what's your position with NASA?

C.B.. Ground crew.

ED. Ah

BETTY. *(to DONNA)* Do you know any of the astronauts?

DONNA. Yes Ma'am. *(pointing to the wall)* They signed that picture for me.

BETTY. *(to ED)* Honey, look, that's their picture.

ED. I see it.

BETTY. *(to DONNA)* What does it say?

DONNA. "To Donna".

BETTY. To Donna.

ED. Uh-huh.

BETTY. Do you know the teacher? Is she nice?

DONNA. Oh yeah, she's a real good lady.

ED. *(to C.B.)* So what do you do on the ground crew?

C.B.. Right now, too much.

BETTY. It must be exciting, though, to send people up to space.

C.B.. Oh yeah.

ED. Anything interesting going up? In payload?

C.B.. Well, we got a communications satellite and some gizmo that's gonna measure the comet. But we've / got something going up next month...

BETTY. We're going back to Arizona to see the comet.

C.B.. Oh, uh-huh. Is that where you're from?

BETTY. No, we're from / Oregon.

ED. Oregon.

C.B.. Uh-huh.

BETTY. Ed took an early retirement and we sold our house and bought a Winnebago.

ED. I worked in engineering...

BETTY. We're traveling now. Ed loves to take pictures.

ED. I have an interest in photography...

BETTY. We started down the coast of California and we saw the Redwoods and the Gold Country and the Wine Country and then we went to San Francisco and saw the Golden Gate Bridge...

ED. A nice piece of construction...

BETTY. It's just beautiful.

ED. Got some nice shots of it in the fog...

BETTY. And then we went to Carmel in time for the butterflies...

ED. Monarch. They migrate once a year...

BETTY. And then in Big Sur we saw the whales. And then we saw Hearst Castle which was unbelievable...

ED. A lot of money went into that project.

BETTY. And then we went to Los Angeles and took the studio tours which were a lot of fun.

ED. They had a demonstration of special effects...

BETTY. And then we went over to New Mexico. I wanted to see the pueblos and Ed wanted to visit the atomic bomb site.

And then we went up to Arizona to see the Grand Canyon / which was just magnificent...

(*Over this,* **ED** *wanders over to* **MONET** *and watches him sketch.*)

ED. (*to* **MONET**, *re:* **BETTY**) That's a very good likeness. You got her expression.

(He makes a yammering motion with his hand.)

BETTY. Then we went to Montana and went over to Yellowstone and saw Big Faithful.

ED. Old Faithful.

BETTY. Whatever.

C.B.. So how long you been traveling?

BETTY. Oh eight or / nine months.

ED. Eight and a half months. A long time.

BETTY. We're trying to see everything. Ed has been taking hundreds of pictures.

ED. I have about a hundred rolls so far.

BETTY. I don't know who's going to look at them.

(ED looks to MONET for support.)

But anyway...we've been having quite a time.

ED. *(to C.B.)* The Winnebago's been holding up very well. It's a good piece of machinery.

C.B.. Uh-huh, I hear that.

BETTY. *(to DONNA)* I'd love to go into space, wouldn't you?

DONNA. No way, I'm afraid of heights.

BETTY. So is Ed.

ED. No I'm not.

BETTY. I read that someone's already setting up tours to go into space. Is that true?

ED. It's a scam.

BETTY. No it isn't. They're doing it through Abacrombie and Fitch, I think.

DONNA. It's possible.

ED. *(to C.B.)* I hear they're sending a telescope up.

C.B. Oh yeah. Oh yeah, it's one powerful puppy. It's gonna see fifty times deeper into space than anything we've had before. *(holding up his beer bottle)* It can read the label on this Bud from three thousand miles away.

BETTY. Isn't that / something?

ED. When's it going up?

C.B.. Right after this launch. See, us trying to look at the stars from earth is like a bug trying to look at this room from the bottom of a can of Coke. But with that thing up in orbit, we're gonna see things we don't even know are out there…stars and galaxies and nebulae. And we're gonna see other planets, man. And we're not talking about planets from our solar system, we're talking about the planets around Alpha Centauri and the North Star. Some of them planets might look a little bit like Earth. Some of them might even have life.

BETTY. *(in a hushed voice)* Oh my, can you imagine?

C.B.. We're gonna be seeing deep, I'm talking deep space. We're gonna see the light from stars that are twelve billion years old. We're gonna be seeing the creation of the universe.

(A long pause while everyone takes this in. C.B. looks to see if DONNA has been listening to him. She has.)

ED. This is one fine time to be alive.

C.B.. That's a fuckin' understatement. *(to BETTY)* 'Scuse me.

BETTY. That's all right.

ED. Well, time to turn in. *(to DONNA)* Miss, the check?

(C.B. drains his beer and turns to DONNA.)

C.B.. Guess I better get some sleep.

DONNA. Yeah, I guess you better.

BETTY. *(to C.B.)* We think what you people are doing is just wonderful. We'll be rooting for you.

C.B.. Thank you, Ma'am. Goodnight.

DONNA. *(to C.B.)* Hey. I'll see you later.

C.B. *smiles and leaves.*

BETTY. *(to MONET)* Are you a writer?

MONET. No. I paint.

ED. *(to BETTY)* Come on, old gal. Time to hit the hay.

BETTY. Honey, he paints.

ED. I know. *(nodding to* **MONET***)* G'night.

SCENE SIX

(Lights up on **ELIZABETH**. *She is holding a toy space shuttle.)*

ELIZABETH. That Christmas, I had asked my mother for a Cabbage Patch Doll. But she didn't have time to get me one. All the presents she got us that year were from the NASA gift shop.

(The **TEACHER** *joins* **ELIZABETH**.*)*

She gave me a plastic space shuttle and a package of astronaut ice cream.

TEACHER. *(to* **ELIZABETH***)* See? It's freeze-dried!

ELIZABETH. My mother was going to read me *How the Grinch Stole Christmas* but she kept getting phone calls.

TEACHER. *(into phone)* Hello! How are you!

ELIZABETH. While she talked on the phone, I played with the shuttle.

*(***ELIZABETH** *bangs the shuttle on the floor.)*

TEACHER. *(into phone)* I'm going back next week. I'm having the time of my life...hold on. *(to* **ELIZABETH***)* Honey, what are you doing?

ELIZABETH. *(to* **TEACHER***)* I'm trying something. *(to audience)* I was trying to break the wing.

TEACHER. *(back to phone)* It's a real madhouse here. We have the family tomorrow. I thought I'd cook a roast.

ELIZABETH. Too many people were coming to the house.

TEACHER. No, thank you, we have tons of food. I keep telling everyone, if I gain anymore weight they'll have to add extra fuel just to get me off the ground.

ELIZABETH. She kept saying the same thing over and over again.

TEACHER. Well, as I've been telling everyone, I'm more nervous about getting in the car and driving on the freeway. It's a chance in a lifetime. I wouldn't miss it for the world.

(**ELIZABETH** *starts banging again.*)

TEACHER. *(cont.)* Excuse me. *(to* **ELIZABETH***)* Elizabeth, would you please stop?

(**ELIZABETH** *throws the shuttle across the stage.*)

(into phone) Can I call you back?

(The **TEACHER** *hangs up and turns to* **ELIZABETH***.)*

Pick that up.

(**ELIZABETH** *shuffles over to the shuttle and picks it up.*)

What's gotten into you?

ELIZABETH. Nothing. *(to audience)* She was talking on the phone too much.

TEACHER. Honey, are you bored?

ELIZABETH. I hated the shuttle.

TEACHER. Do you want Daddy to take you out with the sled?

ELIZABETH. I hated space.

TEACHER. Do you need a hug?

ELIZABETH. I think at that moment, I hated her.

TEACHER. Honey, come here.

(**ELIZABETH** *goes to the* **TEACHER**, *lets herself be held.*)

Does that feel better?

(**ELIZABETH** *starts banging the shuttle against the side of her leg.*)

Do you want to tell me what's wrong?

ELIZABETH. *(weepy)* I can't find my coloring book.

TEACHER. Is it in your room?

ELIZABETH. *(still banging the shuttle)* No.

TEACHER. *(stopping* **ELIZABETH***'s hand)* Honey, don't. Did you look under the tree?

ELIZABETH. No, it's not there. Somebody took it.

TEACHER. Maybe your brother has seen it. Did you ask him?

ELIZABETH. *(furious)* I don't want to ask him.

*(The phone rings. **ELIZABETH** starts banging the shuttle again. The **TEACHER** stops her hand again.)*

TEACHER. Elizabeth, don't do that, please.

*(**ELIZABETH** yanks one of the wheels off the shuttle, turns around and throws it at her mother.)*

All right, that enough. Go to your room.

ELIZABETH. *(to audience)* I went to my room and later I came out and apologized. My mother forgave me. She blamed my behavior on Christmas.

TEACHER. *(into phone)* It's Christmas. You know how they get all wound up.

ELIZABETH. She took me to bed and was going to read to me about the Grinch but she got another phone call.

(phone rings)

TEACHER. Hello! How are you!

ELIZABETH. My father tried to finish the story for me.

TEACHER. *(into phone)* I'm having the time of my life...I go back next week.

ELIZABETH. I got mad and tore a page in the book. He turned the light out and told me to go to sleep.

TEACHER. *(into phone)* I'm trying not to gain any more weight. They'll have to add extra fuel just to get me off the ground...well, as I've been telling everyone...

TEACHER & ELIZABETH. I'm more nervous about getting in the car and driving on the freeway.

ELIZABETH. It's a chance in a lifetime.

TEACHER. It's a chance in a lifetime.

TEACHER & ELIZABETH. I wouldn't miss it for the world.

SCENE SEVEN

(Projection: the stained glass Rose Window of Chartres Cathedral.)

(lights up on TEACHER*)*

TEACHER. Even if you were very poor, you were free to walk into the cathedral and look up at something as magnificent as this. People came from hundreds of miles around on something called a pilgrimage. Can anyone tell me what it must have been like to be a pilgrim and to walk into a cathedral like Chartres?

(a beat)

Can anyone tell me what must have gone through your mind if you had never been outside your own village and you lived in a stone hut without any windows and you couldn't read or write and you spent your days pulling a plow through the mud and you slept in the same room with your pigs and you walked two hundred miles over primitive, rocky roads in a pair of sandals that started giving you blisters after the first day and you ran out of food and a band of robbers stole your last coin and no one would even offer you a ride, and finally, finally you arrived at the cathedral and you saw this?

(She motions to the projection.)

Anyone? *(a beat)* Jason? *(a beat)* Yes, many people were burned at the stake. *(a beat)* Yes, alive. Can we talk about that later? Heather?

(The projection changes to a picture of a reliquary.)

Most cathedrals were built around a patron saint. And some of these cathedrals contained something called a relic which was held in this, a reliquary. Can someone tell me what a relic is? *(a beat)* Patricia? *(a beat)* That's right, a relic is a piece of the body of someone believed to be a saint. It could be a piece of bone, or some hair or even a fingernail.

TEACHER. *(cont.)* *(a beat)* Yes, it is gross, but back then people believed that these remnants were—well, blessed. That if you touched them, you would be close to God. Patricia? *(a beat)* Well, my feeling is that most of the saints were ordinary people who happened to have been put in extraordinary situations. I think it's what people said about them later on that turned them into saints. But then again, they might have been, as you said, of God. Jason? *(a beat)* Yes, many of the saints suffered terrible deaths. Unfortunately that is one of the things that qualified a person to be a saint. In any case—can anyone think of a modern example of a relic? Anything that held some kind of magic for you? *(a beat)* No one? Well, remember when we took that trip down to the Air and Space Museum and we stood in line to touch the moon rock? Do you remember how exciting it was to touch something that had come from the surface of the moon? Mathew? *(a beat)* Well, I know we've been to the moon many times and brought back many rocks. But it's still a miracle that we did it at all, don't you think?

(long beat)

No? Oh, well then how many of you are going to fly to the moon for your summer vacation? Anyone? No? All right, then how many of you know someone who's been to the moon—your grandparents, a neighbor, a friend? No? All right then, one last question. If you were given the chance, how many of you would like to go to the moon?

(The **TEACHER** *waits. We see shadows of hands appear in front of the projection as one-by-one, the children raise their hands.)*

SCENE EIGHT

(The bar. **DONNA** *and the* **TEACHER** *are standing on either side of a bar stool.)*

TEACHER. Go ahead.

DONNA. Go ahead what.

TEACHER. Climb up.

DONNA. Uh-uh, no way.

TEACHER. What could happen?

DONNA. This thing could tip over, I could break my head.

TEACHER. You won't fall, I'll hold on to you.

DONNA. Uh-uh, can't do it.

TEACHER. Chicken.

DONNA. Hey, this is how I am. I'm an earth sign. I don't have any problem with my phobia. If I have to reach something high, I don't need a ladder, I get my boyfriend to do it.

TEACHER. What if he's not around?

DONNA. I get another boyfriend. Look, I get along very well. My sister, she sent me a plane ticket to visit her in Pittsburgh. I said no thank you, I can drive. It only took me a day to get there. I was relaxed. I was alive. I don't need planes. Forget planes. Planes crash.

TEACHER. Oh come on, and cars don't? That is / so lame–

DONNA. I just read in the paper the other day about some jet / taking a dive off the runway –

TEACHER. How often do you get your car serviced?

DONNA. On my salary? Honey, if it ain't broke.

TEACHER. Tell me about it. I had to get a new set of tires. Five hundred dollars.

DONNA. No way.

TEACHER. I could have gotten the cheaper ones, but the man at the garage said if I'm going to be driving my kids around…

DONNA. That's how they get you.

TEACHER. He's right, if it was just me in the car–

DONNA. No, I hear you.

TEACHER. But to get back to my point, that flying–

DONNA. Here she goes.

TEACHER. –flying is much safer than driving because a jet is not allowed to leave the ground until every moving part is checked.

DONNA. Oh come on, do you think the ground crew at an airport is really doing their job? Those guys are looking at jets all day, they get bored with the routine, their minds are wandering all over the place. They're thinking about their girlfriends, what they're gonna have for lunch. They're gonna get sloppy. Even the ground crew here, they're the creme de la creme, but they screw up all the time –

(The TEACHER *looks at her.)*

–Oh Honey, that's not what I was trying to say. I was just–that was just me going along with the argument. I don't even know where that came from. Listen, these boys have their hearts and souls wrapped up in those rockets. I swear to the Lord, they'd rather cut their own throats than let anything happen to you.

(The TEACHER *just nods.)*

You want a drink?

(The TEACHER *shakes her head.)*

You want to put me up on this stool? I scare the crap out of you, you get to scare the crap out of me, an even exchange? So what do I do?

TEACHER. Take my hand.

DONNA. All right.

(The TEACHER *helps* DONNA *up on the stool.)*

I'm too big for this.

TEACHER. No you aren't.

DONNA. I'm gonna fall.

TEACHER. I have you.

> (**DONNA** *is now standing on the stool but is still bent over in a panic.*)

Straighten up.

DONNA. Don't let go.

TEACHER. I won't. Keep your eyes open, keep looking up.

> (**DONNA** *slowly straightens up.*)

That's a girl. All right, I'm going to let go of your hand.

> (*The* **TEACHER** *does so.* **DONNA** *is standing by herself on the stool.*)

DONNA. OK I did it, thank you, let me down now.

TEACHER. Not yet.

DONNA. I don't like where this is going.

TEACHER. Reach your hand up, try to touch the ceiling.

DONNA. Damn, why am I listening to you?

TEACHER. Because I'm the Teacher. Come on. Reach.

> (**DONNA** *reaches her hand up, touches the ceiling. She puts her hand down.*)

How are you doing?

DONNA. I'm doing OK.

TEACHER. Just stay up there for a minute and take in the view.

DONNA. All right. *(a beat)* Oh man, there's a bunch of dead bugs on top of the TV. What'd you send me up here for? Get me down, I don't need to look at that.

> (*The* **TEACHER** *helps her down.*)

I'm gonna send you up there next time. Send you up with a broom, clean all that shit out…hey, are you all right.

> (*The* **TEACHER** *holds her hands up. They're shaking.*)

Oh man, is it that thing that I said? Come on sit down.

> (**DONNA** *moves behind the bar.*)

DONNA. *(cont.)* What do you take, gingerale?

TEACHER. I wet my pants in training today.

DONNA. Oh don't worry about that, happens to the regulars all the time. Which ride did they put you on?

TEACHER. The escape basket.

DONNA. The one with the twenty story drop?

TEACHER. Straight down, eighty miles per hour.

DONNA. Oh yeah, I know about that one.

(**DONNA** *hands the* **TEACHER** *her drink.*)

TEACHER. They told me to keep my eyes open.

DONNA. *(snorts)* What for, the scenery?

TEACHER. I kept my eyes on my knees.

DONNA. That's the thing to do.

TEACHER. But I still lost control of myself. I was so freaked out, I didn't know my seat was wet until they pulled me out of the cage.

DONNA. There's no shame in it, Honey. Astronauts are always messing in their pants. The men who went to the moon? The whole time they were up there they were shuffling around in dirty diapers. When they came back down and they opened up that capsule? Whoo, step back!

TEACHER. It's all still very primitive, isn't it?

DONNA. Naw, it's much better now. The moon landing, they didn't know what they were doing. They got up there with duct tape and prayers. These days–they've sent enough of them up, they pretty much have it down.

TEACHER. Should I be praying?

DONNA. You're asking me? Please, I pray every time I get in an elevator.

TEACHER. Do the astronauts pray?

DONNA. I always pray for them. I've never lost one yet.

TEACHER. I prayed to be chosen to go up.

DONNA. Well, there you go.

SCENE NINE

(lights up on **ELIZABETH***)*

ELIZABETH. I had lost my mother once before. It was at the supermarket.

(The **TEACHER** *appears, pushing a grocery cart.)*

It was late in the day and it was very crowded. I remember begging my mother to give me a quarter so I could get a super ball from the gum machine. She wanted me to stay with her and help her pick out some cereal. So I went with her to the cereal section and pointed to the Lucky Charms. But she decided we should get…

TEACHER. Nutri Grain.

ELIZABETH. She said I would like it because it had raisins.

TEACHER. Honey, you'll like it. It has raisins.

ELIZABETH. She also got a box of granola bars.

TEACHER. You can have one in the car.

ELIZABETH. Her right hand had blue magic marker on the middle finger. She kept good care of her nails, but her fingers were always marked up with pen. She was wearing a plaid dress. I followed her to the meat department. The butcher was busy and we had to wait. I asked again for the quarter so I could buy a super ball from the gum machine. *(to* **TEACHER***)* Mommy, please?

TEACHER. Honey, why do you want a super ball?

ELIZABETH. Because I need it. Please?

TEACHER. It's part of your allowance.

ELIZABETH. I don't care. *(to audience)* She dug in the pocket of her dress and pulled out a quarter.

(The **TEACHER** *hands her a quarter.)*

It was warm. I left her to go the gum machine. The machine with the super balls was broken so I put my quarter in a machine that had creepy-crawlys. I got a green scorpion and I hated it. I went back to the meat department but my mother was gone. I went up and down the aisles, looking for her plaid dress. Mom? Mom? I listened for my mother to call back but all I could hear was the supermarket music playing, "Rain drops on roses, and whiskers on kittens…" Mommy? Mommy?

(**BETTY** *comes on with a cart.*)

ELIZABETH. *(cont.)* I saw a woman in a plaid dress bending down by the soups. *(to **BETTY**)* Mommy?

BETTY. What do you want, little girl?

ELIZABETH. I ran to the check-out counters and went from register to register looking for my mom. I saw a box of Nutri-grain moving on a conveyor belt.

(**ED** *is standing in line.*)

But the Nutri Grain was followed by a bag of prunes and an old man was pulling out his wallet. I ran to the parking lot to see if my mother was in the car. But a man came through with a bunch of carts.

(**C.B.** *comes barreling towards her with a stack of carts.*)

C.B.. Coming through! Coming through!

ELIZABETH. And he didn't' see me and he almost ran me over and I started to cry. I ran back to the check-out counters and I saw a little girl standing there with her mother. And her mother handed her a granola bar. And I knew I would never have a granola bar again because I went to the gum ball machine and got a green scorpion which I hated and I didn't even have the quarter my mother gave me which was still warm from the pocket of her dress, the quarter that my mother's hand had touched with the magic marker on the middle finger, I lost it. I knew that she was gone. I knew that she had left without me and I would never, ever see her again.

(crying hysterically)

ELIZABETH. *(cont.)* MOMMEEEEEE! MOMMEEEEE! I WANT MY MOMMEEEE! GIVE ME BACK MY MOMMY!!!!

(The **TEACHER** *passes by with her cart.)*

TEACHER. Elizabeth?

ELIZABETH. Mommy, I couldn't find you! I looked everywhere! You were gone! I thought you went home! I thought you left me!

TEACHER. Silly, why would I leave without you? Why would I do that?

*(***ELIZABETH** *is still sobbing. The* **TEACHER** *holds her.)*

We'll be home in a little while.

ELIZABETH. I stayed very close to the cart.

*(***ELIZABETH** *puts her hand on the handle next to the* **TEACHER***'s hand. They start pushing the cart together across the stage.)*

And when we got in the car, she gave me a granola bar.

SCENE TEN

(Lights up on **BETTY** *and* **ED**. *Sound of the ocean and an occasional gull.* **BETTY** *is sitting in a plastic lawn chair.* **ED** *is setting up his camera on a tripod. Apart from them is* **MONET**, *painting at his easel.* **BETTY** *keeps looking over at him, desperately wanting to see what he's painting.)*

BETTY. Are you here for the launch?

MONET. Yes.

BETTY. Are you from around here?

MONET. No, I am from France.

BETTY. France. Oh, I've always wanted to go to France. I love the Impressionists, don't you?

MONET. You know of them?

BETTY. Oh yes. Ed and I saw the Van Gogh exhibit in New York. I bought some of his note cards.

MONET. Van Gogh?

BETTY. He did that famous painting, "Starry Starry Night?"

MONET. Yes, I know of him.

*(**BETTY** looks at what he's painting.)*

BETTY. You're very good.

MONET. Thank you.

BETTY. You know, if I had tried to paint that scene I would have made it all gray and brown. But look at all those colors. Do you actually see those colors or do you make them up?

MONET. No, Madame, they are all there.

BETTY. *(to* **ED***)* Honey, you should see what he's doing. He's very good.

ED. Betty, I'm sure the man would like to be left alone. *(to* **MONET***)* She does the same thing to me when I'm trying to take a photograph. She's always telling me where to point.

BETTY. Well, sometimes you need direction. *(to* **MONET***)* He takes too many pictures of horizons.

ED. Horizons are a good point of reference, am I right?

MONET. They are hard to ignore. But there comes a time when you have to let them go.

> *(***ED*** watches* **MONET** *paint for a beat.)*

ED. *(shyly)* I used to paint. Water colors. I would of liked to have done it full time, but well, you know…

MONET. I understand.

ED. I still have the eye for it though. *(squinting up at the sky)* That's one heck of a blue, isn't it?

MONET. It most certainly is.

BETTY. *(to* **MONET***)* Wouldn't you just love to paint from outer space?

MONET. Very much.

BETTY. You know, once when Ed and I flew cross-country, I spent the whole time looking out the window. It was the most beautiful view I'd ever seen. I loved the farm land – all those fields in different colored squares. It looked like a giant patch-work quilt. I kept thinking to myself, "wouldn't it be wonderful if someone like Van Gogh were sitting next to me and he could look out the window and see what I'm seeing." Has that ever occurred to you?

MONET. About Van Gogh? No.

ED. Betty, have you seen my lens paper?

BETTY. Did you check the glove compartment?

ED. Yes.

BETTY. What about your camera case?

ED. That's where it was supposed to be.

BETTY. Well, Honey, I don't know.

MONET. I believe it's in your coat pocket next to your glasses.

> *(***ED*** checks his coat and pulls out the lens paper.)*

ED. Well, I'll be.

*(**MONET** begins to pack up his easel.)*

BETTY. If you want to keep painting, we'll let you alone.

MONET. I am done for now.

BETTY. The launch is about to start. Don't you want to stick around?

MONET. It won't happen today.

*(He takes **BETTY**'s hand and kisses it.)*

It was a pleasure, Madame. I will try to do as well as your Mr. Van Gogh. *(to **ED**)* A friend of mine, Victor Hugo, once said: "The horizontal is the line of reason, the vertical is the line of prayer." Don't worry about your horizons. Someday, you won't even know it, they will disappear.

SCENE ELEVEN

ELIZABETH. I remember a reporter asked me what I thought of my mother going into space. I didn't want to answer so I hid my face behind my grandmother's purse. My brother laughed at me so I hit him on the arm. My grandmother gave us Lifesavers to quiet us down. I told her I wanted a cherry so she peeled the paper down until she found one for me. I put it in my pocket for later. Then my mother joined us and she let me hold her hand while she talked to the reporters. I played with her wedding ring and I was very proud that I was one of the few people who was allowed to touch her hand. She showed the reporters some of the things she was taking up to space. She had a journal and in the journal was a bookmark that I made for her. I had drawn a rocket and stars and Saturn with the rings and I ironed it between two pieces of wax paper so it would be protected from the gamma rays. Then she showed the reporters something her class had given her. I was jealous and I wanted to give her something else. So I took out the Lifesaver. It was fuzzy from the lining of my pocket. While my mother and the reporters talked, I tried to make the Lifesaver presentable. I told myself that I had to pick all the lint off the Lifesaver or my mother wouldn't come back. Finally my mother crouched down next to me. She was wearing her blue space suit. I touched the patches on her shoulders. She looked so beautiful. Suddenly I couldn't grasp that this woman was the same person who every morning sliced banana on my granola. My grandmother kept saying, "say good-bye, honey, say good-bye to your mother." But all I could manage to do was to hold out the Lifesaver which was sticky from the sweat of my hand. My mother took it and put it in her pocket and I knew that everything would be all right.

SCENE TWELVE

*(Lights up on the **TEACHER** strapped into her shuttle chair which is angled all the way back in the take-off position so that she's flat on her back. She's dozing.)*

NASA VOICE ON SHUTTLE RADIO. ...T-minus thirty minutes and counting. Checking fuel valves.

*(**MONET** appears, carrying his portable easel and paint box. He's holding a book mark.)*

MONET. Madame? Madame, you dropped this.

TEACHER. *(waking)* Oh, thank you. Are we in space yet?

MONET. No, not yet.

TEACHER. What am I thinking, everything would be floating by now, wouldn't it. You aren't floating, are you?

MONET. Only in time, Madame.

TEACHER. Are you coming with us?

MONET. I plan to, yes. *(his easel)* Do you know where I might put this?

TEACHER. Oh gosh, I'm not sure. They don't give you a lot of storage space in here. Are those your paints?

MONET. Yes.

TEACHER. I might have room in my locker for a couple of your tubes but I don't think you'll be able to take your easel. You won't really need it up there anyway.

MONET. No, of course I won't. How silly of me.

TEACHER. *(the bookmark)* Did you see this? My little girl made it for me.

MONET. Yes, it's quite marvelous. *(reading)* E-li-za-beth.

TEACHER. Oh my God, I didn't see that. She wrote her name. You don't know what a big thing this is for her. I've been trying to help her learn it but she said she couldn't because I gave her a name with too many letters in it. She gets so frustrated, she always tears up the paper. This is such a big step for her. Oh my sweet girl. I should have paid more attention when she gave it to me.

NASA VOICE ON SHUTTLE RADIO. T-minus twenty-eight minutes and counting. Fuel system is functioning.

TEACHER. Is there a phone up here? I have to call her. I have to call her or she'll think I didn't care.

(*The* TEACHER *tries to unbuckle herself.*)

I can't get out of this. Can you help me?

MONET. I will try but I'm afraid that I'm not very mechanical.

TEACHER. Please hurry, I need to get out of here.

MONET. I am trying, Madame.

TEACHER. I need to see her. I need to see my little girl.

NASA VOICE ON SHUTTLE RADIO. T-minus twenty-six minutes and counting. Checking auxiliary wing flaps.

MONET. I'm so sorry, but I cannot open the buckle.

NASA VOICE ON SHUTTLE RADIO. Auxiliary wing flaps are functioning. Checking main wing flaps.

TEACHER. Oh God, will she ever forgive me?

MONET. Do not despair, Madame.

NASA VOICE ON SHUTTLE RADIO. T-minus twenty-four minutes and counting. Main wing flaps are functioning. Checking right tail flaps.

(MONET *has left. The book mark slips out of the* TEACHER*'s hand and falls to the ground.*)

Right tail flaps are functioning. Checking left tail flaps.

(*The* TEACHER *tries to retrieve the bookmark but she can't reach because of the restraints.*)

(*lights start to fade*)

Left tail flaps are functioning, checking rudder…

SCENE THIRTEEN

(Fade up on **BETTY** *and* **ED** *on the beach waiting for the launch.* **ED** *is making last-minute adjustments on his camera which is set up on a tripod.* **BETTY** *is listening to a portable radio.)*

NASA VOICE ON RADIO. ...T minus 15 seconds and counting.../no unexpected errors.

BETTY. Do you think it will actually go up this time?

ED. Well, I'll believe it when I see it.

NASA VOICE ON RADIO. T-minus 14...13...12...11.../10... 9...8...7...6...5...we have main engine start...

BETTY. *(over this)* Where are we supposed to be looking?

ED. It should be coming up about twenty degrees to the south.

BETTY. That doesn't mean anything to me, Ed. Do I look straight ahead or to the right, or what?

ED. *(pointing impatiently)* Over there, just look over there.

NASA VOICE ON RADIO. *(over this)* ...4...3...2...1...and lift off. We have lift off of the twenty-fifth space shuttle mission. And it has cleared the tower.

*(***ED*** looks through his camera, starts clicking. We hear the distant roar of a rocket.)*

BETTY. There it is! I see it! Oh my God! Look at it! Oh Ed, look at it go!

*(***ED*** is madly clicking and advancing the film.)*

ASTRONAUT VOICE ON RADIO. Houston, we have roll program.

NASA VOICE ON RADIO. Roger, roll Challenger.

BETTY. Isn't it beautiful! It's just beautiful! How do they do it?! Oh my God, it's just magnificent.

NASA VOICE ON RADIO. Challenger, go with throttle up.

ASTRONAUT VOICE ON RADIO. Roger, go with throttle up.

(an explosion)

(**BETTY** *looks puzzled.* **ED** *looks up from his camera.*)

BETTY. Was that supposed to be part of it?

NASA VOICE ON RADIO. One minute, 15 seconds. Velocity 2,900 feet per second. Altitude nine nautical miles. Downrange distance seven nautical miles.

BETTY. *(over this)* Are they all right?

(**ED** *doesn't say anything, stares at the sky.*)

Oh my God, oh Ed, my God. Oh my God.

(**ED** *puts his arm around* **BETTY** *and leads her off. Then:*)

NASA VOICE. Flight controller here looking very carefully at the situation. Obviously a major malfunction.

SCENE FOURTEEN

(Lights up on the TEACHER. *She is facing the kids holding a cage with a dead guinea pig inside.)*

TEACHER. All right, everybody let's quiet down. That's enough. Let's try to find out what happened here.

C.B.. I think I figured out what happened here.

TEACHER. Five of you were responsible for feeding Miss Piggy.

C.B.. Sixteen thousand of us were responsible for getting one rocket into space.

TEACHER. All right, who had Monday? Heather was supposed to be Monday.

C.B.. And all of us were divided into different departments, see? And every department was divided up into divisions and minidivisions and mini-mini divisions.

TEACHER. Heather, if you forgot to feed Miss Piggy on Monday, then you should have told the person on Tuesday so they could have given her extra food. Who had Tuesday? One at a time!

C.B.. And every division had it's own technical language, see. For instance, there's this little plastic part the size of my pinkie.

TEACHER. All right, Matthew was sick on Tuesday. And what about Wednesday? Anyone?

C.B.. The guys in tiles and O-rings call it a "C-scale Oxidizer."

TEACHER. Who was Thursday? Jennifer?

C.B.. The guys in air locks call it "an OMS Regulator." And over in propulsion they call it a "Preburner Fuel Thrust."

TEACHER. Someone told you it was for every other week?

C.B.. Hell, I just call it a valve.

TEACHER. Who was Friday? *(a beat)* I never said I was Friday. Did I?

C.B.. So this is the point. See, it's just like the Tower of Babel.

TEACHER. Has anyone heard of the Tower of Babel? *(to a boy)* Jeffrey, can you tell us?

C.B.. OK, a long time ago everyone in the world was gonna get together and build this big tower, right? They were building it 'cause they were trying to reach heaven. And they started building this thing and it was goin' really well and it got higher and higher. And God got really nervous and He...

TEACHER. Or She, go on...

C.B.. ...wanted to figure out a way to stop them.

TEACHER. That's right.

C.B.. So God made all the people who were working on the tower...

TEACHER & C.B.. ...speak in different languages.

TEACHER. And the people who sawed the wood couldn't understand the people who mixed the mortar.

C.B.. And the guys in mortar couldn't understand the guys in brick. And the guys in brick couldn't understand the guys in drywall and everyone started running around and...

TEACHER & C.B.. ...shouting at each other and no one knew who was supposed to do what, and everyone started making mistakes (fucking up)...

TEACHER. ...and the wrong nail was put in the wrong board...

C.B.. ...and the wrong board was hammered to the wrong beam.

TEACHER & C.B.. And the whole thing came crashing down.

C.B.. The whole damn thing came down.

TEACHER. We have to speak clearly to each other. Or else, look what happens?

(She holds up the cage.)

C.B.. That's what happened.

TEACHER. Jennifer, would you take Miss Piggy to the janitor?

C.B.. ...too many damn departments. But it was still my fault.

TEACHER. No, Jason, you can not have the bones.

SCENE FIFTEEN

(Lights up on **C.B.** *holding a letter.)*

C.B.. *(reading)* "Dear Elizabeth, I'm writing to you on behalf of the men who worked on the ground crew of shuttle flight 51-L. We want you to know how much all of us admired your mother and we offer our sincerest condolences to you and your family."

(He puts the letter down.)

I volunteered to write this letter 'cause I feel partly responsible for what happened. I don't know what you remember, but there were a lot of false starts before your mom's ship finally got off the ground. Some of the delays had to do with the weather, but one of the delays had to do with human error. This human error delay took place on a day that would of been perfect for a lift off. The weather was clear and the sky was a beautiful bright blue. It was as if God just lifted up a giant man-hole cover and said "aim here." Well, at T minus nine minutes they couldn't get the handle off of one of the hatches and they had to get this special drill. But when that arrived it didn't work 'cause someone used it and didn't bother to replace the batteries. Let me just explain the situation. See, I borrowed the drill to fix the door on my van. So after work I used the drill then I stuck a note on it saying to change the batteries. But I used a post-it that I took off someone's door and the sticky stuff on the back was kinda used up and I guess it didn't stay on the drill. I should of just changed the batteries myself but in order to do that I would of had to fill out a form explaining why I needed the new batteries and then I'd have to run it over to another building to get it approved, then wait an hour to have it processed then run to another building to pick the batteries up, then I would of had to get a guy to supervise me while I put the batteries in and hell, I was at the end of a twenty hour shift of regulating a bunch of LOX bleed valves and my next shift was in five hours. So instead I went to a local place to wind down. It's a place where a lot of us hung out with your mom and the other astronauts. Once, I played her a game of darts. She beat the heck out of me. You would of been proud. She also won the football pool. What I'm trying to say here is that we saw your mom every day. The last thing any of us wanted to do was to send her up in a ship that was gonna fall apart. I'm sorry. I'm so sorry. I never meant to take your mommy away from you.

(going back to the letter)

C.B. *(cont.)* "She was a great example to us all and will live long in our memories as a pioneer of our times. We extend our best wishes for your future and hope that as your mother did, you will be able to follow your dreams. Sincerely Yours, C.B. Williams and the men of Ground Crew number 7749, Division Eighty-six, Department K699-99, Kennedy Space Center.

SCENE SIXTEEN

(Sound of ocean and helicopters. Lights up on **BETTY**
and **ED** *beach combing.* **MONET** *is drawing in the sand
with his staff.)*

BETTY. *(to* **MONET***)* Apparently this is a good beach for
scraps. This man told us that he used to come down
here during the Mercury program when they were
testing all those rockets? He said the darn things were
blowing up every other day and they'd fall in the
ocean and the tide would bring them up right here.
He said he'd come here and pick up the pieces and
then bring them home and mount them on plaques.
I thought it was a little strange, but as Ed explained it
it's like owning a little /piece of history.

ED. A little piece of history.

*(***ED** *is examining something.)*

BETTY. Honey, what is that? Do you have something?

ED. I don't know.

BETTY. *(taking it)* Let's see. It's kind of rubbery isn't it?
Maybe it's a piece of the shuttle. Oh my God, it is.
Look Ed, that's what it is.

ED. No, I think it's a piece of a rubber thong.

BETTY. Oh. Oh well.

(she tosses it)

(to **MONET***)* You know what upsets me so much about
what happened? It wasn't only the loss of those
wonderful lives–every time I think about them I want
to weep–but what makes me very sad is that I now know
that Ed and I will never take a trip to space. All those
things that we thought were going to happen, they're
out of our lifetime now.

*(***MONET** *picks something up.)*

BETTY. *(cont.)* Did you find something? Let's see. *(examines it)* Huh. No it isn't anything. It's just a lifesaver.

(She walks away. **MONET** *puts the lifesaver in his pocket.)*

SCENE SEVENTEEN

(Lights up on the bar. **DONNA** *is cleaning up.* **C.B.** *is drunk.)*

C.B.. P.F. Flyers. Do you remember those?

DONNA. Uh-huh.

C.B.. If you put them on you could fly. Remember that?

DONNA. Oh yeah.

C.B.. I remember the TV ad. They showed a kid putting on a pair of P.F. Flyers and then he'd walk out of the shoe store and jump over a building. We believed it. Every kid who watched that ad believed it. I jumped off a roof in a pair of those shoes. Those fucking shoes. I knew a kid who got himself killed 'cause of those God damn shoes.

DONNA. C., I'm closing up soon.

C.B.. They're scrapping the telescope, did I tell you that?

DONNA. Yeah, you did. I'm gonna drive you home, OK?

C.B.. No, I'm fine.

DONNA. You're in no condition, Hon.

C.B.. I gotta get rid of my van. The fuckin' door fell off again, did I tell you?

DONNA. Yes, you did.

C.B.. I killed seven people to fix that door and the God damn thing fell off, can you dig that?

DONNA. Listen, Sugar, I hate to be the one to tell you, but you're not that important. You had nothing to do with what happened. Maybe there are a few puny things down here that you can control, but there's a master plan out there that you can't change, let alone read. Maybe we weren't meant to send that telescope up. Maybe there's something out there God doesn't want us to see. Maybe He thinks we just aren't ready.

C.B.. I wouldn't of screwed up if you let me get my sleep that night.

DONNA. Excuse me?

(**C.B.** *doesn't say anything.*)

DONNA. *(cont.)* How dare you? Don't you go putting blame on my head. You want to climb on the cross for this one go ahead, but I'm not having any part of it. You understand? I've had it with you tonight. I'm locking up. Go call yourself a cab.

(**DONNA** *pushes* **C.B.** *off his bar stool.*)

(*He walks off.*)

(**DONNA** *turns to the audience.*)

A reporter came in here, wanted to know, what was the last thing the astronauts said to me. What did they say to me?, I said. Yes, he said, exactly what did each of them say to you that last night when they left the bar? *(a beat)* "Goodnight Donna," "Goodnight," "Night." "Goodnight Donna." "Night, Donna," "Goodnight." – was that seven? Oh right, one more, "Good night." He actually wrote all of that down. Then he wanted to know if I remembered anything else they might have said to me, it didn't have to be that particular night, "any little tidbits," he said I said, Honey, a tidbit is something you feed to a dog. He then amended himself, asked, did any of them confide in me. Yes they did, I said, but confide comes from confidential and it will remain that way. I could see the hair in his ears start to vibrate with excitement, ooh, this lady has tidbits! How am I gonna get them out of her? He decides to distract me, he looks over at the picture I have of my astronauts, What's that?, he says. It was such a dumb-ass question I didn't even bother to answer, just kept wiping the bar. You must have felt very close to all of them, he said. I just kept wiping.

Then he leaned in towards me, real close, trying to get into some confidence with me, he says, do you think they knew? I just kept wiping and wiping the bar until he went away.

(a beat)

DONNA. *(cont.)* One of my astronauts noticed that I keep a bible behind the bar. And this individual sat with me late one night and we talked about the afterlife. This individual was experiencing a moment of fear. This individual had doubts. I told this individual what I believe to be the truth: that the one thing we know about death, is that we all got to do it. And when and where we do it is left in the hands of God. And those who do it go on to a much higher place than those who are left behind. Those who do it are released of their bonds. Those who do it will finally know the secrets of the universe. And isn't that after all why some fool would want to put themselves on top of a rocket in the first place?

SCENE EIGHTEEN

(lights up on **ELIZABETH***)*

ELIZABETH. When I watched my mother's ship take off, I saw it go straight into the sky and disappear. When my grandmother told me that my mother went to heaven, I thought that heaven was a part of outer space. I was excited because I thought she'd come back with all kinds of neat presents like a plastic harp or a pair of angel wings. I went to the mailbox every day looking for a post card from her that would have clouds on it or a three-D picture of God. I waited for her to call long distance. When I didn't hear from her, I got very angry. I told my father that I hated her for being away so long. He told me that she had "perished" in the rocket. I told him that wasn't true, that she was alive. That she had left us and found a family that she liked better. He asked me why did I think she was still alive. And I said, "because I never saw her dead." These are the reasons I gave myself for why my mother didn't come back. One: I hit my brother on the arm. Two: I wouldn't talk to the reporters. Three: I didn't say thank you to my Grandma for giving me the coloring book. Four: I wouldn't let my father hold me. And five: I didn't get all the lint off the Lifesaver.

*(***ELIZABETH*** sits on the floor in front of the TV with her crayons and the scribbled drawing we saw earlier.)*

TV NEWSCASTER. *(voice over)* Reports today from NASA have given us new evidence on the Shuttle disaster. The cockpit has been recovered and the bodies have been found.

*(***MONET*** enters and turns the TV off.* **ELIZABETH** *looks at him. He looks down at what she's been drawing.)*

MONET. Ah. Spaghetti?

SCENE NINETEEN

(Projection of one of Monet's paintings of the gardens at Giverny.)

(Lights up on MONET *and* ELIZABETH. MONET *hands her a bouquet of flowers.)*

MONET. My mother was a wonderful gardener. When I was a little boy I used to help her. I got a half a *centime* for every snail I killed. She had every kind of flower imaginable. Hollyhocks and columbine, tulips, lilies, pansies, sweet William, forget-me-nots. Her favorite flowers were poppies. They were very big, very bright. Orange and red. Fantastic colors. She told me, "Claude, the secret to poppies is to plant them firmly in the ground. If the roots are firmly set, then the flowers will grow tall. And never water them from above or the flowers will be weighted down by the drops which would defeat the purpose of the poppy, because the purpose of the poppy is to float above the other flowers. They are nature's balloons." Whenever I would cut them, I held tightly on to the stems for fear that they would float away. My mother died when I was ten. She caught pneumonia while trying to tie up some roses during a storm. her last words to me were, "I love you Claude...don't forget the snails." After she died, I wouldn't have anything to do with her garden. In two weeks, the snails had chewed everything down to the stems. My mother's garden was lost. I took great pains to punish myself for my neglect. I went to confession. I wouldn't take dessert. I wore my woolen coat without a shirt. I offered to cut my father's toenails. But the next Spring, everything started to bloom again. I killed the snails and I brought my mother's garden back to life. One day in late Spring, the sun was warming the air and the most wonderful perfume rose up from the garden. It was my mother's scent. And I felt my mother bending next to me, guiding my hand as I dug in the earth. And I felt her breath in my ear, and she whispered, "Claude, always turn the soil in the spring, don't hurt the worms, feed the roses twice a year and please, don't ever water poppies from the top."

(**MONET** *digs in his pocket and pulls out the lifesaver. He carefully picks a piece of lint off then hands it to* **ELIZABETH**.)

(**C.B.** *runs shouting and whooping across the stage.*)

C.B.. It's up! They got it up! God damn! They got the telescope up! We're gonna see to the edge of the universe! OOOOOOWHEEEEEEEEEEEEE!

SCENE TWENTY

(A projection of the Horsehead Nebulae.)

(C.B. and DONNA sitting on a swing. A large telescope is floating in front of them. C.B. guides the eyepiece down to DONNA so she can look through it.)

C.B.. No, I'm serious, I want you to see this.

DONNA. Hon, I know this star gazin' shit from high school.

C.B.. Oh man, you have a one-track mind, you know that?

DONNA. Just lookin' after my own shop, Sugar.

C.B.. Hey Lady, what makes you think you're more interesting than what I can see in this 'scope? Huh? Here, take a look. OK, you see in the upper left hand corner of that dark part that looks kinda like a horse?

DONNA. *(looking)* A horse...you mean a whole horse?

C.B.. No, just his head.

DONNA. Oh, OK, I see it...

C.B.. Now just to the right, on his nose, is that real bright part?

DONNA. Uh-huh...

C.B.. Now count three stars up from that. *(a beat)* You have it?

DONNA. Uh-huh, I think so...

C.B.. The third star to the right...take a look at it.

DONNA. I'm looking...

C.B.. You see anything around that star?

DONNA. Not yet...

C.B.. Keep looking.

(DONNA suddenly gasps)

DONNA. Oh my God.

C.B.. Pretty amazing isn't it?

DONNA. C.B., oh my God.

C.B.. You're the first one I've shown it to.

DONNA. I can't believe it.

C.B.. I wanted you to see it.

DONNA. It's blue. And it has clouds.

C.B.. Yep, just like ours.

DONNA. I can see oceans. And land...

C.B.. Kinda pretty, isn't it?

DONNA. It's like a beautiful blue marble. It's out there. Oh my God.

C.B.. I named it after you. Donna. The planet Donna.

DONNA. *(shouting up at the sky)* Hello! We see you! Hello!

C.B.. HELLO!

DONNA & C.B.. Hellooo! HELLOOOOOOO!

(As lights fade on **C.B.** *and* **DONNA,** *the projection dissolves to a shot of the Earth from space.)*

SCENE TWENTY-ONE

(The projection changes to another shot of the Earth as seen from the surface of the Moon.)

(Projection changes to an out-of-focus shot of the Moon.)

*(Lights up on **BETTY** and **ED** sitting in their lawn chairs in front of the screen. **ED** has one of those automatic slide changes in his hand. He clicks it.)*

(Projection: another fuzzy shot of the Moon.)

BETTY. Ed, how many of these did you take?

(Click. Projection: another bad shot.)

Honey, I thought you sorted these.

(Click. Projection: another bad shot.)

ED. *(to audience)* Let's see, I think this one was from the Sea of Tranquillity.

(Click. Projection: an out-of-focus Earth rising over the moon.)

BETTY. Honey, what happened?

ED. I was trying a different lens.

(Click. Projection: the famous picture of footprints on the Moon.)

That's a shot of man's first step on the moon.

BETTY. *(to audience)* He bought that one.

*(Click. Projection: a shot of **BETTY** floating.)*

Oh, now this is me in our hotel room. It orbits the Earth every twenty minutes.

ED. Ninety minutes.

BETTY. Ninety minutes. We stayed in the zero-gravity wing of the hotel. They don't have any beds in the room. You just shut your eyes and float. Ed was always dozing off.

ED. Well, you tired me out. *(to audience)* You get a lot of honeymooners up there.

BETTY. *(embarrassed)* Well, of course, that too.

ED. *(to audience)* Would you like to know what it's like?

BETTY. Ed, stop.

ED. *(to* **BETTY***)* They'd like to know.

BETTY. I don't think so.

ED. *(to audience)* It was the best experience in our marriage that we ever had.

BETTY. It was very nice.

ED. That's not what you said to me.

BETTY. Well. *(to audience)* At first it was silly. It was very silly.

ED. *(to audience)* It takes some practice. You can't make any sudden moves.

BETTY. It can be dangerous. I almost killed poor Ed.

ED. That's right, she almost killed me.

BETTY. I accidentally kicked his leg and he went sailing into the air lock hatch. *(to Ed)* You remember our clothes?

ED. That was pretty wild

BETTY. *(to audience)* We didn't put our clothes away so they just hung there –

ED. In mid air.

BETTY. And the more we moved, the more the clothes would tumble around.

ED. Tumble around.

BETTY. And they kept tangling up in our feet. It was like being inside a giant washing machine.

ED. It's like being under water.

BETTY. That's right, under water.

ED. Betty looked like a mermaid.

BETTY. Oh, stop.

ED. Her hair was floating out from her head and her bosooms…

BETTY. Ed…

ED. …her bosooms had a life of their own.

BETTY. You thought I was funny-looking. You should have seen what you looked like.

ED. I didn't say you were funny-looking. You were beautiful.

BETTY. So anyway….

ED. Anyway…

BETTY. It was very silly.

ED. But once we figured out what we were doing…

BETTY. Honey, they've heard enough.

ED. You see, on Earth, everything is horizontal or vertical but in space it's 3-D. Even with a bad back the variety is endless.

BETTY. Ed.

ED. What was it you said to me?

BETTY. I don't remember.

ED. Betty said, the best thing about making love in outer space is that you don't have to worry about who's on top.

BETTY. It's true.

(**BETTY** *takes* **ED***'s hand.*)

We had two windows in the room. On one side we looked out at space. On the other side we looked down at the Earth. Ed held me and we watched the sun set and then a few minutes later, we saw it rise again.

And on the other side was the whole universe spread out before us with the brightest stars we'd ever seen. We were suspended next to each other, very still, feeling no weight. Like we weren't two people anymore but two spirits…

ED. Two spirits…

BETTY. Who had floated up from Earth.

SCENE TWENTY-TWO

(Projection: Monet's Water Lilies. It dissolves into a shot of the Earth taken from the shuttle–a vista of clouds scattered across land and ocean. The patterns of the clouds blend in with the brush strokes of the painting.)

(lights up on **MONET***)*

MONET. I had to master the conditions of space before I could start to paint. One can't simply throw one's brush down and pick up another as you do on Earth, as anything you put aside will float away. But thanks to a wonderful material called Velcro, I've been able to keep my tubes fastened to my smock. However I do tend to lose track of the caps and must hunt them down like butterflies when I'm done. The paint itself is thick enough so that if I'm careful it will stay adhered to the palette. But sometimes in my enthusiasm I will squeeze a tube too hard and the paint will float away from me in the form of a brightly colored snake. The view outside the window is quite intriguing. There is no horizon line to speak of. Just patterns of clouds and land and sea and a clear, fantastic light. Every ninety minutes we circle the Earth and I have the pleasure of watching sixteen sunsets a day. My only regret is that it passes by so fast. When I painted my series of the cathedral, I used to be enormously frustrated with the rapid change of light but the time I had then was luxurious compared to what I have now. So I've lined up six canvasses in a row and I work on each section of the Earth as we sail by. And when we pass into night I load up my palette with paint so I'm ready to start back on canvas number one. I have fifteen orbits in which to finish my paintings until the Earth shifts into another time of day. I plan to paint every piece of Earth in every kind of light. I'm very much looking forward to seeing the Mediterranean at sunrise and I hear that the French Alps are quite spectacular at dusk. I have been painting for four straight days now. I have no desire to eat or sleep. My body is no longer of consequence. I have only eyes and a hand and a brush and paint and the sun endlessly bouncing colors off the Earth. And I will continue to paint as long as this wonderful rocket will keep me in space.

SCENE TWENTY-THREE

(lights up on **ELIZABETH**

ELIZABETH. About a year after my mother died my father took us to the Mingus Family Circus. Even at that age my brother and I could tell it was a pretty raunchy operation. The men who set up the tents and shoveled the elephant poop all had tattoos and bad teeth. My brother told me they were all drug addicts. We saw one of them throwing up behind a trailer. At intermission I stayed in the tent and watched them set up the trapeze for the high wire act.

(Over the following, **C.B.** *and* **ED** *play the roustabouts. They roll a very tall ladder on to the stage.)*

About a dozen of them ran around fitting metal poles into the ground and hoisting lines of rope. I saw two of them trying to keep a giant metal pole taut against the wires. It wasn't long enough so they stuck a rubber tire under it. That didn't work so they kept slipping pieces of wood between the tire and the pole, like you slip match books under a table leg to keep it from wobbling. I thought maybe I should tell someone about this but then the lights dimmed and my brother pulled me back to my seat.

*(***MONET** *steps out, wearing a top hat.)*

(Tacky circus music starts to play.)

MONET. Ladies and Gentlemen, Boys and Girls, if you will direct your attention to above the ring, the Mingus Family Circus proudly presents the Fearless First Family of Flight, the Flying Hernandez!

ELIZABETH. And then the Hernandezes came out, dressed in blue tights and sparkles and smiling and waving. They were nice looking people. I wanted to run up and grab them and shout, "Don't fly! Don't fly! Something will happen, don't fly!" But I just sat there and ate my brother's popcorn and watched as the Flying

Hernandezes shed their capes and climbed up the ropes. As the first Hernandez stepped up on the tiny platform, thirty feet above, I waited for the wood to crack and send him hurling to the ground. And when that didn't happen, I watched as the head Hernandez grabbed the trapeze and swung out. I knew that the wires would snap and send him sailing through the top of the tent, leaving a hole in the canvas in the shape of his body. And when that didn't happen, I knew that we were only waiting for the biggest disaster of all.

MONET. Ladies and Gentlemen if I can have your attention please. The Flying Hernandez are about to perform their famous simultaneous triple somersault. We request that you please remain absolutely silent for the duration of their act.

(a drum roll)

ELIZABETH. Everyone in the tent was still. The only thing that was moving was the head Hernandez who was swinging back and forth by his knees and flexing his hands.I wondered if he knew about the rubber tire and the wooden blocks. I wondered if he knew that they were all about to be killed.

(drum roll continues for a beat, then TA-DA)

But it didn't happen. The head Hernandez was now sitting on his trapeze, swinging back and forth like a kid at a playground. And I realized that something truly remarkable had just happened. That despite the bad rigging and the degenerate ground crew, the Hernandezes were still alive. And it was at that point that the Head Hernandez looked down at me and said…

MONET. Come up, come on up!

ELIZABETH. And that's when I accepted that we were meant to fly.

*(**MONET** leads **ELIZABETH** to the ladder and she slowly starts to climb it.)*

NASA VOICE. T minus ten…nine…eight…seven…six…we have main engine start…

(spot on **C.B.** *and* **DONNA** *watching a TV over the bar)*

…four…three…two…one…

(Spot on **ED** *and* **BETTY** *standing on the beach, looking up.)*

…and lift-off and we have lift-off of the twenty-fifth space shuttle mission. And it has cleared the tower.

*(***ELIZABETH** *continues to climb the ladder)*

ASTRONAUT VOICE. Houston, we have roll program.

NASA VOICE. Roger, roll Challenger.

ASTRONAUT VOICE. Velocity 2,257 feet per second. Altitude 4.3 nautical miles. We have three good APU's. Downrange distance three nautical miles.

NASA VOICE. Challenger, go with throttle up.

*(***ELIZABETH** *has reached the top of the ladder. She holds the lifesaver up, hoping to stop the inevitable.)*

ASTRONAUT VOICE. Roger, go with throttle up.

(a beat)

Welcome to space, guys.

(The **TEACHER** *is above her in her NASA coveralls, blowing bubbles.)*

TEACHER. Now the reason I'm doing this is to show that bubbles will still hold their shape in outer space. But the one difference is that soap bubbles on earth will burst after a few seconds, but bubbles in space can last for a couple of centuries. Unless, of course, one of the other astronauts bumps into them. Now the reason I'm weightless is because we are in zero-gravity. Gravity is the force that pulls us towards the center of the Earth. There is also another definition of gravity.

(A dictionary comes floating by. The Teacher opens it to a place marked by a Post-It.)

TEACHER. *(cont.)* Let's see…Gravity. *(reading)* "Graveness or seriousness; solemnity, heaviness."

(The TEACHER *closes the dictionary and lets it float away.)*

If someone told me a year ago that I'd be doing somersaults in outer space I would have told them it was impossible. I don't use that word anymore. Because whatever seems impossible now will be possible later on. It could happen in your lifetime or it could happen for someone two hundred years from now. I will never see all the miracles of mankind but one miracle is enough for me to know that anything we dream, anything is possible. OK, they're signaling to me to wind this up. The other astronauts have to get back to work now. Um, hello to everyone down there. Hello to my class and hello to my family. Elizabeth, eat your granola. I love you. I'm having a wonderful time up here. I really am. Please don't anyone stop on my account. It's all right. Go on.

END OF PLAY

COSTUMES

ELIZABETH
Jeans w. belt, shirt, corduroy shirt
High-top sneakers

TEACHER
Plaid dress w. red sweater
Shoes with hose
Earrings, ring, watch
Scene 4: Remove red sweater
Scene 10: NASA flight suit w. Space Center patches/Boots
Scene 11: Add NASA helmet
Scene 13: Remove helmet

DONNA
Jean shorts w. belt, t-shirt
White shoes w. socks
Jewelry, watch
Apron
Scarf
Scene 19: Remove apron

BETTY
Reversible jacket (solid showing), blouse, plaid pants
Sneakers w. socks
Ring
Scene 9: Reversible jacket (plaid showing)
Scene 10: Remove jacket/Add vest and sun hat
Scene 12: Remove beach apparel/ Add jacket, wool hat, mittens
Scene 15: Remove jacket, hat, mittens

ED
Tan trousers w. belt, polo shirt, windbreaker
Boat shoes w. socks
Ring and watch
Scene 10: Add cap
Scene 12: Remove cap/Add wool scarf, hat, mittens
Scene 15: Remove scarf, hat, mittens
Scene 20: Remove windbreaker

C. B.

T-shirt, navy coveralls w. Space Center patch

Boots

Navy NASA cap

MONET

Shirt, tie, tan check trousers, suspenders, linen jacket, vest

Straw hat

Handkerchief

Lace-up shoes w. socks

Colored pocket square

Scene 5: Remove hat

Scene 10: Remove jacket

Scene 11: Add linen jacket and straw hat

Scene 18: Remove pocket square/ Add silk top hat, silk scarf and white gloves

Scene 21: Black jacket, vest and trousers

CREW MEMBERS

Royal blue coveralls w. Space Center patches

Shoes

PROPERTY PLOT

STAGE RIGHT

phone

drawing

guinea pig cage

slide clicker

rubber thing

lens paper

lifesavers

3 shopping carts

black stool

radio

chair

tripod

Monet mobile w. shuttle chair (head facing downstage)

ladder

crash helmet w. visor down

beach chair

easel and bundle w. folding stool and paint box

beach bag w. lotion (Betty)

blanket (Betty)

bar with bar stool upstage side; on bar: full bottle of beer, bowl w. popcorn, caddy, open rag, receipt pad, pen; in bar: tub w. water and small pocket w. 3 stacks of glasses

can of ginger ale

bottle of wine, 1/8 full

beer bottle, 1/2 full

glass of scotch, nearly empty

remote control

adding machine

receipts

inventory list

pen

velcroed blacks

teacher's stool

circus ladder

STAGE LEFT

circus drum

1 shopping cart

2 chairs

2 tables

steering wheel

2 glasses w. ginger ale

toy shuttle

camera

pamphlet

purse w. sunglasses (Betty)

Monet palette

rag

2 white brushes

sketch pad

drawing pencil

pencil sharpener

bookmark

easel w. painting

HOUSE RIGHT

chair

2 stacked bar stools

red basket

PERSONAL PROPS

letter (C.B.)

wallet w. money, sunglasses, lens paper (Ed)

bookmark in inside jacket pocket (Monet)

SET

Bare stage with set pieces